HUNTING DOWN THE HEIRESS

DOG DETECTIVE - THE BEAGLE MYSTERIES BOOK 3

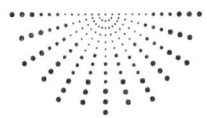

AGATHA PARKER

ROSIE SAMS

SWEETBOOKHUB.COM

©Copyright 2020 Agatha Parker

All Rights Reserved
Agatha Parker

License Notes
This Book is licensed for personal enjoyment only. It may not be resold. Your continued respect for author's rights is appreciated.

This story is a work of fiction; any resemblance to people is purely coincidence. All places, names, events, businesses, etc. are used in a fictional manner. All characters are from the imagination of the author.

Agatha is a member of SweetBookHub.com, a place where you can find amazing fun books that are sweet and suitable for all ages. Join the exclusive newsletter and get 3 free books here

THE DOG DETECTIVES – THE BEAGLE MYSTERIES

Welcome to my book. I recently joined forces with the amazing Rosie Sams to work on this wonderful series of cozy mystery books all featuring a sweet little Beagle puppy. Mazie is an ex-police dog who was wounded in service. She is gifted to Hannah Barry, a broken-hearted realtor who is down on her luck.

At first, Hannah is unsure, can she learn to love the Beagle? What will she do when a body is found?

Find out how Mazie found a new home and Hannah some peace in book one of this series Sniffing out the killer each book can be read alone.

Rosie has a free book Smudge and the Stolen Puppies that you can pick up. It is about an amazing and cute French Bulldog the best Dog Detective in all of Port Warren. Grab it here for FREE

CHAPTER ONE

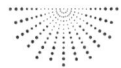

Hannah felt the crisp fall air in Blairstown, Vermont, edge toward chilly. Winter was in the air. The frequency of her walks with her beloved pup, Mazie, had decreased as the weather turned cooler. Plus, she had less time to spend taking in the architectural details of the houses she once loved to observe. All of her time recently had been devoted to her career switch. She had moved away from being a realtor and had started the process of becoming a private investigator. It was a move she never would have considered, had it not been for her good friend, Colin Troughton.

She pulled her car into a parking spot in front of her favorite coffee shop, Jolt of Java. Opening the door to the store, she took in the delicious smell of the beans being freshly roasted in the back. A familiar comfort moved through her bones as she maneuvered toward her spot, a table by the stone fireplace. The warm flames were crackling and inviting her over. She sat down, hoisting her purse, bursting with papers and files, on to the seat next to her and glanced around; she couldn't wait to catch a glimpse of Anita and Oscar, it had been so long.

"Hannah!" came a friendly voice. Anita had spotted her almost immediately. Taking off her apron, she popped out from behind the counter and walked toward Hannah. "Oh, it's so nice to see you, it's been far too long since you were here!" Anita bent down to give Hannah a squeeze around her neck.

Hannah smiled up at her friend. "I've missed you, Anita. We have so much to catch up on. How are things?"

Anita scooted Hannah's hefty purse out of the way. "Never mind about me," she replied. "Nothing's going on here beyond coffee and Oscar, mix and repeat. I want to hear all that you have been up to." She placed a loving hand on Hannah's arm and held her gaze. "You've been next to impossible to get a hold of. I've been calling and texting... I was starting to worry."

Hannah gave a tired smile, but her eyes sparkled. "I'm sorry. I know I haven't been around so much. I've been so busy... working out all the details to become a private investigator took longer than I expected!" She paused, waiting for the news to sink in. She'd floated the idea past Anita and Oscar, but hadn't confirmed that she would definitely be doing it. "There was a lot to do and learn, but I've loved every second of it."

Anita furrowed her brows together. She glanced up at Oscar behind the counter and motioned for him to come over.

Her husband, Oscar, told the teenaged barista that he'd be back in five minutes and walked over to meet with the ladies. "Hannah! Long time no see, what's new with you?" he reached down to give her a hug, making a conspiratorial face at his wife when Hannah couldn't see.

"Hi, Oscar, so good to see you too," Hanna replied. "I think I mentioned that I was going to shift gears and move away from being a realtor last time I saw you?

Well, I'm following through – I've been studying to get my PI license, and have even secured new office space for it! I've been busy trying to get everything in order." She smiled at him expectantly, then added, "I'm sorry I've been such a stranger. I'll try to be better."

Anita kicked her husband's shoe beneath the coffee table. Oscar cleared his throat. "Ah, that does sound like it would keep you occupied." Anita made a face at him, so he pushed on. "But, Hannah. Are you sure you want to give up being a realtor completely? It didn't feel like so long ago when you were sitting at this same table, studying hard to get *that* license," he said, carefully.

Hannah looked from Oscar to Anita, surprised that they were less than supportive.

Then Anita jumped in, less carefully. "Hannah, how can you just throw in the towel? You have worked so hard for your real estate career!" she spoke passionately with her hands joining in.

Then the realization settled into Hanna. "You two don't think I can do this?" she asked, hurt creeping into her voice.

Anita softened. "It's not that we don't think you can. We are your biggest fans," she replied. "It's that we don't know if you *should*. Things were really starting to pick up for you with real estate."

Hannah nodded. "I understand your perspective. Really. But – especially after watching how sophisticated Francis Garland and Kerry Dorson are, I came to realize that I'd only ever be an average realtor. I don't think I want to be just okay at something for the rest of my life. I figured there had to be more," she explained. "After solving two crimes, and with a little push from Colin, I realized what my true passion, even skill is; being a detective." She paused to let her words rest. "And I hope that you can both support me in this new endeavor," she finished.

"Of course, Hannah," Anita replied. "We will support you in anything. We just aren't sure if..."

Oscar swooped in, hoping to soften the delivery. "We just think maybe you should keep your options open. Maybe sell a few houses while you get set up as a P.I."

Hannah nodded, hurt by their seeming lack of

confidence in her. "I see." She gathered her purse, suddenly feeling that she wasn't in the mood for a coffee. "It was really nice to see you both. I need to get back to walk Mazie, she's been in the house alone all day." She stood up and gave her friends a tight smile. They both rose to give her hugs, which she reluctantly accepted. She left the coffee shop and hopped in her car. She told herself to keep it together until they couldn't see her anymore. As she turned the corner away from the Jolt of Java, she let the tears fall.

When she pulled into the driveway of her cozy home, Mazie's little face was peeking out at her from the front room. The tri-colored beagle was barking frantically as a greeting, excited to see her owner. Hannah opened the front door and accepted every lick Mazie had to offer.

"Let's go for a walk, girl!" she said, slipping the wiggling beagle into her harness. Fresh air and her dog always made her feel better. Together they made their way down the quaint city sidewalk. Hannah watched Mazie's happy tail move from side to side. Every wag of her tail seemed to indicate that she was on Hannah's side and the little dog's joy was contagious. Hannah couldn't help but smile in response.

The two of them hadn't walked more than two blocks when they ran into a familiar face. Hannah recognized the tall, muscular frame heading in their direction, and her face lit up. "Colin!" she greeted him with a dazzling smile.

Colin's green eyes glinted when he saw Hannah. "Hannah, fancy meeting you here." He gave her a kiss on the cheek. "And Mazie, hello, little buddy," he reached down and gave Mazie a pat on her head.

"Any updates on your restaurant?" Hannah asked.

"We are just putting the finishing touches to it now," he replied. "All of the permits came through last week, so we are full speed ahead. Sorry about all the noise, by the way. I hope it hasn't bothered you too much." Colin, a developer from New York, was following his dream of opening a restaurant in town. It just so happened that his new business was positioned right next to Hannah's new office space.

"It's not been a bother at all," Hannah said. "In fact, all of the activity has given me the inspiration to move things along in the P.I. department!"

"I'd love to take a look at your progress," Colin said. "I've never been inside of an official P.I. office before." The smile he gave her was enough to make her toes curl, the man was attractive.

Hannah had been working hard on getting her new business up and running, but the office space hadn't made much progress so far. She emitted a little laugh. "Why not? Since it's on your way," she said.

With that, Hannah, Colin, and Mazie all set off to check out her new office space.

CHAPTER TWO

Hannah and Colin smiled together at the sight of Mazie's happily wagging tail as the trio walked along the sidewalks of the rural town. They passed by Colin's restaurant first. "Would you like to pop in and take a look?" he asked.

"I was hoping you'd offer," Hannah replied with a grin.

Colin held the door for Hannah and Mazie and lead them on a tour of the space. It was looking every inch like an upscale eatery. There were solid oak tables, fine art on the walls, gorgeous light fixtures, and soft mood lighting already installed. "This is fantastic," Hannah gushed. "I knew you were talented in the kitchen, but I didn't realize you also had a penchant for interior design."

"I just had a clear vision," he replied. "And a lot of help. I had to hire a designer to execute the ideas. My gifting is much more in the culinary arts than interior design, that's for sure."

"I had a feeling that anything you touched turned to gold, and this seems to be no exception," Hannah said, smiling shyly at him.

"That's kind of you to say. And it means a lot, coming from you." Colin moved a few steps closer to Hannah. She felt her breath catch as she stared up into his emerald green eyes.

"Why don't we go check out my space?" she offered quickly.

"I'd love that."

They ventured the few steps down the sidewalk to her office next door for a tour of Hannah's building. She turned the key to unlock the front door and pushed it open. "Here we are!" she said proudly and flicked the light switch on, illuminating her new space.

Colin glanced around and seemed to be speechless. "Wow." He looked at Hannah, noting her pride. "This is... this is sure something!" he managed.

Following his eyes, as they looked around the room, she saw the multiple boxes, still taped shut with a layer of dust over them. The slightly lopsided single desk with chipped paint which had been salvaged from a second-hand store and only one of the overhead lights had a working bulb. "Have you, uh... have you had much time to spend here?" he asked, hardly able to mask his concern.

Hannah's pride in her new space waned as she heard the doubt in Colin's voice. She looked around her office and saw the situation in a new light. Albeit a dim light. Then she wondered what dust and boxes had to do with being a detective, anyway? "Colin, are you saying that the state of my office will determine whether or not I'll be a successful P.I.?"

He looked alarmed. "Of course not, Hannah. I guess I was just a little surprised to see the space...like... given how long you've been working toward getting things set up." His eyes held concern, and it was obvious that he was now worried that he had hurt her feelings.

"I've been focusing my energy on more practical things, like licensing, training, making sure I'm ready to get out in the field and do things the right way," she said gulping down her hurt. "No one looking for an investigator is going to walk in here and base their decision to hire me on how my office space looks." She scanned the disorganized area once again and pushed the doubt from her mind. "All it will take is the sweep of a broom and a little bit of reorganizing. Maybe an afternoon of elbow grease... tops." She looked at Colin, daring him to disagree.

"I hope you're right," he replied. "And please know that I'm always willing to help out. In fact, I'd love it." He looked in her eyes at this, willing her to hold his gaze. "Remember, if you feel like you've taken on more than you can handle at any point, just let me know!" he urged. "I'm always here."

Hannah appreciated his concern, and his offer to help, but she was also hurt at his insinuations. After all, wasn't *he* the one who encouraged her to pursue this new career path in the first place? "Remember who convinced me to go in this direction before you start too much naysaying," Hannah said.

"I don't think you're hearing me as I'm trying to

come across," Colin argued. "I know you'll be a fantastic P.I. After all, I was able to see you in action during your last two cases. I'm merely suggesting it wouldn't be so bad to ask for help on occasion," he tried again.

Before Hannah could respond, they were interrupted by a knock on the front door. Hannah raised her eyebrows at Colin. "Hmm, who could be knocking on the door of my disorganized office?" she said, heading to answer it.

Colin shook his head, hoping she understood his point of view.

Hannah opened the door to greet a young woman with light brown hair. "Hello there, welcome to Hannah Barry, P.I." she smiled, gesturing for the woman to come inside.

The brunette woman walked in looking very professional in a silk wrap dress and high heels. "Hello. My name is Nadine Murphy."

"Hi Nadine, I'm Hannah," she reached her hand out to shake Nadine's. "How can I help you?"

"I've heard that you were setting up an office in

town," she shuffled her feet together. "And I've got a job for the new P.I." She lifted her eyes to meet Hannah's.

Hannah had to work hard not to look at Colin and give him an, 'I told you so' look; after all, she could do that when Nadine left. "Nadine, you have come to the right place. I'd love to help you," Hannah replied. "Come in and let's talk about your case."

CHAPTER THREE

"Nice to meet you, Nadine," Colin offered his hand for her to shake. "Please, come in and have a seat." He gestured to the threadbare couch that looked to be from the same second-hand shop as the desk. He eyed Nadine with concern that she would be put off by the dusty office space, but she seemed too distraught to notice at all.

Colin and Hannah unfolded two plastic chairs that had been leaning against the wall. Colin gingerly wiped the cobwebs away before sitting down. They sat across from Nadine, eager to hear what she had to say.

Mazie settled near Hannah's feet, alert and protective. Her big, brown eyes stayed focused on the designer leather purse Nadine carried under her arm.

"So, what can you tell us about your situation?" Hannah asked.

Nadine shifted slightly in her seat. She folded one leg over the other and looked at Hannah. "This brings me no comfort to discuss." She looked at Colin, then back again to Hannah. "But my father, Theodore Murphy, came to his Blairstown lake house for his annual summer vacation this year. He's a successful banker in New York and very much looks forward to these trips to decompress from the stress of his job." Nadine fiddled with the strap of her purse.

Hannah nodded as she listened.

"Well. It's now November, as you know. And he is still here. In Blairstown." Nadine seemed to be finished with her story. She folded her hands together and placed them on her knee.

"I see," Hannah said carefully. "And you know where he is? He's not missing?"

"No, no. It's nothing like that. He is very much here

in Blairstown. And he's very much here with Stephanie Thayer," Nadine said, unhappily.

At the mention of Stephanie Thayer's name, Hannah felt a spark of recognition. She felt as though they were getting closer to the issue now. Stephanie was a barmaid at Bryce's Tavern, the watering hole popular with locals. The tavern was positioned on the main street so it also attracted tourists. And Stephanie had a reputation for attracting a certain type of tourist. She was a beautiful blond with an eye-catching figure. Her smile and charm made men think they were the only person in the room. And she turned that charm way up, especially for the wealthy tourists. She had a knack for finding and positioning herself very specifically in front of men who lavished expensive gifts upon her.

"So, your father is in Blairstown with Stephanie Thayer?" Hannah repeated, encouraging Nadine to continue.

"Exactly. And not only is he with her. He is engaged to her!" Nadine said her voice raising with her stress.

"Ah," Hannah replied, as the realization settled in.

"It does sound like you are concerned for your father."

Nadine nodded, wiping away a stray tear.

"And may I ask, what exactly would you like my help with regarding Stephanie Thayer and your father?"

"I don't think Stephanie has the best of intentions for him," Nadine leaned closer to Hannah and lowered her voice. "In fact, I think he may be in grave danger."

"I see," Hannah replied, her pulse quickening at the suggestion. "Why don't I pay a visit to your father. I can poke around a bit, talk to him and Stephanie, and see if I can find anything suspicious?" she offered.

Nadine breathed a dramatic sigh of relief. "That would be fantastic. Thank you so much!" Nadine opened her purse to pull out her wallet. "How much do you need to get started?" she asked.

"Oh, no." Hannah waved her money away. "I need to do some digging around first to see if there is a case to be had. It wouldn't be right for me to take your money before we've determined if there is any validity to the case."

"Oh, I see," Nadine replied, putting her wallet back in her purse. "Well, thank you. I'll write down my father's address for you, along with my phone number." She looked at Hannah for some paper.

"Let me see if I can find something for you," Hannah said, getting up to open the drawers in her desk, only to close them again when she saw that they were empty.

She could see that Colin had to stop himself from shaking his head, he reached into his pocket where he happened to be carrying a pad of paper for his wait staff. He handed it to Nadine.

Hannah thanked him with her eyes from across the room.

Nadine scribbled her information on a scrap piece of paper and handed it back to Hannah. "Thank you so much. Please, do let me know what you come up with," she said as she walked to the door.

When it closed, Colin waited for a beat, but then couldn't help himself. He turned to Hannah. "How will you ever get your business up and running if you offer your services for free?" he asked.

Hannah's head jerked to look at Colin. "Of course, I will charge for my services, but not if there is nothing to investigate. It would be unethical to take money for a dead end." She placed her hands on her hips and glared at him.

"Respectfully, Hannah, I beg to differ. Time is money and you are providing a service," he argued. "Your time is valuable. The time you will spend 'poking around' Theodore's house is worth something." Colin meant his comments to come across as advocating for Hannah, but he was beginning to think they came out as more of a challenge to her sensibilities. He could see from her face that it sparked a flare of annoyance in her.

"Respectfully, Colin. I am fully capable of handling this on my own. I might remind you *again,* that you were the one encouraging me to pursue this in the first place," Hannah said, feeling her blood pressure rise.

Colin looked to the ceiling, concerned he wasn't going to be able to rein the conversation back in. "Hannah, I think you are taking this the wrong way."

"I think I'm taking it the way you are saying it," she

replied. "Now, if you'll excuse me, I'm going to take Mazie for a walk to Theodore's lake house." Hannah clipped Mazie's leash onto her harness and walked toward the door. Just as she grabbed the handle, she turned to look at Colin. The sincerity on his face tugged at her. She let out a little breath. Though she couldn't quite meet his eyes, she asked in a clipped tone, "Colin, would you like to come along?"

Colin looked at Hannah standing by the door and took in her blond hair, her brown eyes flaring and her cheeks flushed with frustration. He couldn't say no to more time with her. He suppressed a smile and rolled his eyes, following her out the door.

CHAPTER FOUR

The brisk wind in the air kept Colin and Hannah's scarves up around their mouths so that they had an excuse not to talk for the first part of their walk. The cool weather seemed to calm their heated tempers down as they walked along for a few blocks, and soon they found themselves in front of a beautiful lake house. The dark blue shingles contrasted with the white trim. The charming home blended into the landscape, highlighting the waterfront view that they could see through the front door, and out of the panoramic living room window.

They knocked on the ornate door and waited. Footsteps approached from the inside of the house, and to their surprise, it was Stephanie Thayer who answered the door. Her long blond hair was swept up in a high ponytail, bouncing with each step she took. She cocked her head to the side and beamed a bright smile at her guests. "Well, hello there!" she chirped. "How can I help you both?"

Hannah hadn't thought as far as what to say when she arrived. Especially if Stephanie answered. She blurted out quickly, "Hi, there! My name is Hannah Barry, and I'm a local realtor in the area."

Stephanie's smile stayed steady, but her eyes scanned Hannah and Colin, taking them both in.

"I know this is unorthodox," Hannah continued, "but we were just admiring your lovely home and wondered if we could take a look around? If it's not an imposition?" She hoped she didn't sound too false.

Colin managed to catch Hannah's eye when Stephanie wasn't looking at him and raised his eyebrows as if to say, WHAT?

"Oh! How kind of you to say!" Stephanie replied. "And I would just love to show you around. This place is fantastic," she cooed. Then she looked down to see Mazie. "And who is this little sweetie?" she asked, crouching down to scratch behind Mazie's ears.

"This is Mazie, my beagle," Hannah replied. We were just out for a walk. She'd be happy to stay outside if you don't allow animals inside."

"Nonsense!" Stephanie replied. "It's far too cold to leave this sweet little pup all alone out here. Plus, I *love* animals. Come on in," she offered, opening the door to them. They were met with a hit of warm air from the heated home, immediately putting them both at ease.

"Theodore!" Stephanie called abruptly. "Theo! We have visitors!" She turned to smile at Colin and Hannah. "Theodore is my fiancé," she said, wagging her left hand in front of them to showcase her new diamond ring.

Hannah was surprised Stephanie could hold her hand up, the diamond on her engagement ring was so huge.

"Congratulations!" Hannah said. "Correct me if I'm wrong, but didn't you used to work at Bryce's Tavern?" she asked.

Stephanie's face lit up. "I did! I loved working there. The clients are the best. In fact, that's where I met Theodore," she said.

Hannah noticed how Stephanie didn't seem at all embarrassed about the fact.

Stephanie began their tour, noting the gorgeous crown molding, the panoramic view of the lake, and the high-end kitchen appliances, fit for a professional chef. A woman in an apron followed them discreetly from one room to the next. By the living room, her presence finally seemed to register with Stephanie who introduced her. "This is Mrs. Lynch. She's been Theodore's housekeeper since, well, forever!" she said.

The housekeeper seemed to stiffen at the comment and looked at them. "It's a pleasure," she said curtly and went back to dusting the shelves.

"Quite the change of pace, then, from barmaid to lady of the manor," Hannah remarked, trying hard to feign a casual tone.

She heard Mrs. Lynch grunt in the background.

Stephanie giggled. "A twist of fate, to be sure. I'm

just so grateful I have my Theodore," she replied. "And you know, Theo is a little, tiny bit older than my usual type, but when Cupid strikes, you don't really have a say in the matter, do you?" she asked, winking at Hannah and glancing toward Colin.

Hannah hoped Colin hadn't seen the look and shook it off. Just in time to distract Hannah, a handsome older man with grey hair appeared. *So, this is what people must mean when they say silver fox*, Hannah thought as she looked at who must be Theodore when he appeared in the doorway of the living room.

Stephanie scurried over to him and draped her arms around his shoulder, pressing her body into his. "Theodore! There you are, baby," she said, smacking baby kisses all over his cheeks.

Hannah noticed Mrs. Lynch cringe behind them at the attention Stephanie lavished on her boss. Mrs. Lynch seemed to be quite the snob, Hannah thought.

Meanwhile, Theodore smiled happily at the affection. "So, who do we have here?" he asked, looking at his guests.

"Hello, there," Hannah said, reaching her hand out for him to shake. "I'm Hannah Barry."

"And I'm Colin Troughton," Colin said, extending his hand.

"And this is Mazie," Hannah said nodding down to her puppy.

"Nice to meet you all," Theodore said with a friendly smile that creased his tanned skin around his eyes. "I do hope you are enjoying our home."

"It's stunning," Hannah replied.

The serenity of the moment was suddenly disrupted by a motor so loud, it seemed to be right there, in the living room. The noise of a Harley reverberated through her chest and set the pictures to rattling on the walls. Then it was gone.

Every head in the room turned to face the front door when a burly man with tattoos trailing down the length of his muscled arms burst into the house. His red hair seemed especially bright – as though there was a fire following him.

"Max!" Stephanie squeaked. "What are you *doing* here?" She moved her body defensively in front of Theodore.

"Who is this?" Hannah whispered to Colin.

Stephanie managed to glance quickly at Hannah so as not to take her eyes off of Max for too long. "This is Max Tolson," she grimaced, turning her gaze back to the intimidating-looking man.

"That's right. I'm Max Tolson," repeated the man with red hair in a deep, throaty voice. "Stephanie's boyfriend." He stood with his arms crossed, glaring at everyone in the living room.

"Ex-boyfriend!" Stephanie corrected.

"Ex today, back on tomorrow, right, Steph?" Max asked, narrowing his eyes toward Stephanie. "I've come to bring you home."

Stephanie looked startled. "Home?" she looked around the room, making deliberate eye contact with Theodore. "Max, this is my home now. I'm here, with Theodore," she said, reaching out to link her arm in Theodore's.

"This old man?" Max spat in disgust. "You can't be happy with a guy like him when you just came from a guy like this," he said, gesturing to his own very fit frame.

Theodore, who was a patient man, looked like he had

had enough at this point and began speaking. "Mr. Tolson, if you will please," he coughed slightly. Once he started coughing it seemed impossible for him to stop. Soon he was doubled over, in a fit of coughs.

"Theodore, please," Stephanie said, ushering him to a leather armchair nearby. "Have a seat and drink this water," she said handing him a glass. She rubbed his back as he drank the liquid down. Then she turned to Max and color flared in her cheeks. "I'm finally with someone who takes the very best care of me. He puts me first, he doesn't argue, he respects my opinion, and best of all," she paused to hold Max's gaze, "he doesn't burst through the front doors of other people's homes."

At this, Max's temper flared, his eyes narrowed and his lips pulled back to reveal gold-filled teeth. He charged at Stephanie, not a split second after she finished speaking.

Colin had been watching Max carefully and saw his sudden movement, matching it with his own as he maneuvered to intercept Max's body with his own before the angry red-head made it across the room.

Mazie wasn't far behind him; running toward Max,

she grabbed his ankle with her teeth, holding on tight.

Colin neutralized Max with a headlock. With his body bent forward he was unable to reach anything. And with Mazie clamped to his ankle, he was helpless.

"Max, I suggest you leave, now, unless you want any more harm to come your way," Hannah said, standing next to him.

Max was still fighting mad. "The only ones who should be worried about harm coming to them are Theodore and this guy!" he said, trying to punch Colin from his position under his arm.

In response, Colin and Mazie wrestled him to the ground, pinning him there.

Hannah whipped out her phone to dial her friend, Kate Carver. The local police chief. "Kate! We need help from law enforcement – we are at Theodore Murphy's lake house. Please, send someone quickly."

Colin kneeled on Max's back, keeping him secure with the help of Mazie nipping at his ankle, as they waited for the police to arrive. Hannah stood next to them with a lamp raised above her shoulders, should the need arise for her to hit Max on the head with it.

Theodore looked on at the scene in his living room, silent and shocked. Stephanie rubbed small circles across his back. She set her jaw and looked determined. "Don't worry, Theodore. I'll see to it that Max does not hurt you in any way."

Mrs. Lynch seemed to have disappeared.

CHAPTER FIVE

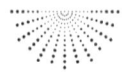

It didn't take long for the police chief, Kate Carver, to arrive with her patrol car lights shining bright. She and her deputy, Ralph Larson, ran swiftly into the living room. Ralph had his gun drawn and Kate spotted Colin and Max right away. She ran over and deftly placed Max's wrists in handcuffs, securing him tightly. Ralph ran over to help hoist Max to standing. "All right, big guy. Let's sit you in the patrol car while we process a few things," Ralph said.

Max, who was not happy to be in handcuffs, marched to the patrol car outside snarling all the time. He struggled to get out of Ralph's grip the whole way, but soon he was securely tucked in the back of the patrol car, fogging up the windows with his anger.

Kate followed them outside. "Let's look him up, see if he has any outstanding warrants or past records. We have him for unlawful entry and attempted aggravated assault, but we want to keep him behind bars long enough to cool off," she said to Ralph.

Ralph nodded and got to work, entering Max's name into the system. Almost immediately a series of unpaid parking tickets and an assault popped onto the screen. "Hey, check this out," he handed the handheld computer out for Kate to see.

"Nice work." Kate smiled. "That'll keep him in there for much longer. I'll go tell the others.

Kate walked into the house to let them know the good news. "We have Max in custody, and he'll be there for a while. Stephanie and Theodore, he won't be bothering you again any time soon."

Stephanie sank into Theodore's side and sighed. "That is fantastic news. Thank you so much!" Theodore leaned into Stephanie slightly, making it clear he had been holding a lot of tension during the exchange. He stood to shake Kate's hand. "Your service is appreciated. Thank you for coming to take care of things so quickly," he said.

When Colin and Hannah saw that everything was settled, they also said their goodbyes. "Thank you for showing us your beautiful home," Hannah said. "And I'm so sorry it ended the way it did."

"Nonsense!" Theodore said. "It was a lucky thing you were here. I'm not sure what would have happened without the help of this strapping young fellow," he said, patting Colin on the back.

Adrenaline was still flying through Colin's body. His hands began shaking as the shock of the moment wore off. "I'm just glad I could be here to help," he said.

"And we can't forget about you, little pup." Stephanie reached down to scratch behind Mazie's ears. "You have a brave little hound here. We would have been in a world of trouble without the help of her securing Max's ankle!"

Hannah beamed with pride on behalf of her dog. "She is a brave one. She actually used to be a police dog, but was injured in the line of duty," Hannah said. "It seems her training hasn't left her!"

"I'll say," Stephanie agreed.

Hannah, Colin, and Mazie left the home, only to run into Mrs. Lynch just outside the front door. "Oh, excuse me. I just wanted to say thank you so much for your help with that Max fellow. You really did save the day there. We all could have been in grave danger without your intervention," she said.

Hannah smiled, noting Mrs. Lynch's guard had come down. Maybe she wasn't such a snob after all.

"It's no problem, it's what anyone would have done," Colin replied.

Mrs. Lynch nodded but pursed her lips. "Yes, well." She looked left to right as if deciding to finish her thought. "You protected us all from a bad situation. But I just can't help but think there may be more danger lurking in the air," she said, sniffing.

Hannah leaned in closer to Mrs. Lynch. "How so?" she asked.

Mrs. Lynch nodded toward the house. "That one in there," she said.

Hannah looked at Colin, wondering if he understood.

"You mean Stephanie?" he clarified.

"Yes," Mrs. Lynch said, crossing her arms.

"It seems Stephanie means well," Colin said, carefully.

"Of course, you would say that!" Mrs. Lynch chirped, turning from him to look at Hannah.

Hannah felt her cheeks warm. "Mrs. Lynch, it really does seem that Stephanie has genuine regard for Theodore. Their affection was very obvious to me."

Mrs. Lynch gave a grunt in response and muttered under her breath "Their union is unholy and only bad will come from it, mark my words." Then she turned to skulk back to the house.

Colin, Hannah, and Mazie were left alone again. "Whew!" Hannah said. "That was quite a tour."

"You're telling me," he said. "I don't know about you, but I could use some food."

Hannah realized that her stomach was growling. And Mazie's tale started wagging at the word. "I could definitely eat," she replied.

"In that case, may I tempt you with a private dinner

at my new establishment, it just so happens I know a guy," he joked.

Hannah ignored her stomach and then looked off into the distance. "Come to think of it, I think I have some leftovers at home."

Colin positioned himself in front of her so she'd have to see him. "Hannah, I wanted to apologize for my antagonistic behavior earlier today, at your office."

Hannah looked at him, softening.

"I shouldn't have chided you for the way you dealt with Nadine. It's your business, and you have every right to do things your own way. I just want to assure you that I'm here to support you, no matter how you want to run things," he finished.

"Thank you, Colin," she said, putting a hand on his shoulder. "I appreciate that. It means a lot," but her eyes still weren't focused on him as they continued on their walk.

"Why do I get the feeling that my apology didn't really help?" he asked.

Hannah shook her head. "No, no. It's not that. I'm

just a little bit preoccupied with what Mrs. Lynch just said, I can't seem to get it out of my head."

"Oh?" Colin urged. "I think she's just jealous."

"Maybe, but I can't help but wonder if there isn't something more to her claims. Stephanie seemed genuine, but Mrs. Lynch sees them when the doors are closed, you know?"

Colin nodded. "Why don't we talk it out at Troughton's Trough?" he offered.

Hannah chuckled, the name of his restaurant providing some levity to her mood. "Troughton's Trough, eh? Do you feel like that name is a little too, 'on the nose'?" Hannah asked.

"Hey," Colin said, bumping her shoulder with his. "You stick to your business, and I'll stick to mine. And we can let the food speak for itself. What do you say – meet me there tonight?"

Hannah bumped Colin's shoulder back.

"Come on, 7:00 P.M., promise?" Colin urged.

"Promise."

CHAPTER SIX

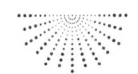

At 7:00 P.M. sharp, Hannah opened the door to Colin's restaurant, Troughton's Trough. At night the interior was even more impressive, with the lights dimmed and the white table cloths starched. Twinkle lights lit the trees and tea lights lit the table for two they shared.

"Will you allow me to order for you?" he asked.

"I'd like that. I guess the owner knows best," she replied.

Hannah sank deeper into pleasure with each dish the server put in front of her. "Hmm, this is exquisite!" she exclaimed with her mouth full of juicy steak.

Colin had his arms folded on the table and leaned in slightly, as though enjoying every second of Hannah's delight in the food. He watched her carefully. Though she seemed to be savoring every bite, she also seemed slightly distracted. "Is everything okay?" he asked.

Hannah swallowed her bite and sighed. She dropped her fork to the side of her plate and leaned in to meet Colin's gaze. "I guess I'm still trying to figure something out."

"What's that?" Colin asked.

"If Mrs. Lynch is still so concerned about what happened, even after Max has been arrested – could there be something else going on?"

"I don't know," Colin replied. "What happened this afternoon would shake anyone up. Maybe she's just rattled by the scene he caused. I must admit, I wouldn't want to mess with too many of his sort."

"Well, there is something else I haven't mentioned," Hannah said.

Colin lifted his brows.

"I called Nadine when I got home, just to let her know what happened this afternoon."

Colin nodded for her to continue.

"Her tune changed very quickly and she asked me to back off the case," Hannah reported.

Colin wasn't sure if that was good news or bad news. "Didn't you get the impression that Theodore and Stephanie were the real deal? I thought you'd be okay to end your investigation?"

Hannah shook her head. "It was the way she asked me. She was almost pleading with me to back off. On the surface, things seem to be resolved, but I have a suspicion there is more going on that I don't know about... yet," she added.

"Hmm," Colin responded. "I can tell that you're going to stick with this one. So, what can I do to help?"

Hannah's eyes brightened. She reached across the table to hold one of his hands. "Will you come with me and Mazie on a walk after dinner?"

Colin narrowed his gaze. "Where would you like to take this walk?" he asked.

"Back to the lake house," she replied.

Colin shook his head, chuckling slightly. "I just have to help clean up after the last service of the evening, but I can join you after that?" he offered.

"No, no," Hannah removed her hand from his. "Please don't rush around for my sake. Mazie and I will be all right to do it on our own. I really just want to ask a few more questions, anyway."

"It's not that, I'd really like to help. To be there with you. But the restaurant is still too new to be leaving it to the staff."

Hannah smiled and patted his hand gently. "I understand! No worries. I'll check in when Mazie and I are back, how's that?" She stood to gather her things. She and Colin hugged goodbye and she went back to her house to collect her trusty four-legged sidekick.

After securing the harness and leash on Mazie, she wrapped herself in her warmest jacket; the setting sun had taken any warmth from the day with it. She even popped a pink and reflective jacket on Mazie so she would be comfortable in the frosty evening air. She secured her wool hat and they hurried to the steps down her porch, both energized to see what else they would discover at the lake house.

They walked briskly toward the house, moving quickly to keep themselves warm. After about twenty minutes, Hannah saw the white trim of the home illuminated in the landscape lights. She followed the cobblestone driveway to the front door. As she lifted her hand to knock, she heard footsteps behind her. She turned to see who it was and saw Colin's tall, athletic frame heading in her direction.

She couldn't help but smile. "Colin! That cleanup didn't take very long."

He reached down to give her a quick embrace. "I rushed through it so I could be here to help you. I didn't love the idea of you being out here alone, at night." He rubbed both sides of her arms up and down quickly in an endearing gesture to warm her up.

She shrugged. "Well, I wouldn't have been completely alone," she said, nodding toward Mazie. "But it's always nice to have you along for the ride," she assured him. They shared a sweet smile and Hannah turned to knock on the door.

After waiting a few minutes with no sign of movement or life in the home, Hannah rang the doorbell. It remained silent. By now, Mazie had started to get antsy, and began sniffing the edges of the patio where they stood. Then she started pulling Hannah on the leash, around the side of the home.

Hannah looked up at Colin. "Should we follow her?" she asked.

"Mazie's nose hasn't let you down yet," Colin said. They both followed behind as Mazie's hound nose sniffed her way to the back of the lake house.

The backyard landscaping was as beautifully lit as the front, with a little crushed stone pathway meandering to the back door. "Look at that," Colin said, pointing to the house.

Hannah followed his gesture to see that the back door was wide open. That was strange in this weather. It was much too cold to have the door open for long.

They ventured closer to the door to see if Theodore or Stephanie were hanging out in the back. When they peaked into the home, they couldn't see anyone.

"Hello?" Hannah called through the door, hoping someone would hear her. She turned to Colin. "Should we go in?"

Colin furrowed his brow. "I'm not sure if we should just barge in there. I don't want to scare anyone," he replied.

Hannah nodded and turned to look at the back yard, hoping to come up with a plan for what to do next. Then she saw the rectangular pool laid out invitingly. The pool lights were not on, though. "Strange," Hannah said. "Every other part of the yard is lit up." The pool drew her and she began to edge closer, studying its dark depths. "Oh, I think someone is in there," she pointed at the dark figure so Colin would see. "Hi, there!" she called out.

Then Colin gasped. Hannah grabbed his arm and moved into his body, letting her eyes focus on the dark figure in the water, and as the reality of what it was sank in she let out a blood-curdling scream.

CHAPTER SEVEN

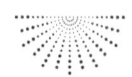

"*T*heodore!" Hannah gasped. Before she knew what was happening, she heard a splash in the water. She looked down to see Colin's shoes sitting empty on the pool deck beside her. He had dived in to try and rescue Theodore, but she knew it was too late. Still, she ran to the side of the pool closest to Theodore to help.

Colin emerged from under the water and pulled Theodore over to Hannah. She grabbed his arms and tried to hoist the body, already water-logged, out of the pool. With great effort and the help of Colin lifting him from the poolside, they were able to drag him, ungracefully, onto the pool deck. Colin lifted himself out of the pool, adrenaline running high so that he didn't feel the cold air on his body.

Hannah turned Theodore on his back and began checking for any sign of breath. "Call 911!" she directed Colin and tilted Theodore's chin up. She breathed into his mouth while plugging his nose, then began chest compressions. His lips were already blue, and she knew her efforts were mostly in vain, but she also knew she had to try. She continued doing CPR until Colin came over to place a hand on her shoulder. "I'm not stopping!" she responded. "Not until the paramedics get here!"

As sure as Colin knew Theodore was dead, he also knew there would be no stopping Hannah. She tried valiantly to revitalize Theodore's lifeless body until her own became too fatigued to continue. She slumped back into Colin's waiting arms when she finally allowed herself to admit he was gone.

Colin comforted her while Mazie began sniffing Theodore, nudging his body with her nose in an effort to rouse him.

"Trust me, Mazie," Hannah said. "He's gone."

Mazie continued to sniff the body until Hannah got

up to help shoo her away. Then Mazie scampered to the other side of the pool, sniffing as she went.

"Mazie!" she called, getting up to corral her dog. "Come here!" Mazie reluctantly obeyed Hannah and came back to her.

Hannah turned to Colin. "How do you think he ended up in here? He's fully clothed. It doesn't seem like it was an accident. No one goes for a night swim without lights and in their clothes. Right?" She was feeling so shocked by the events of the night, that she was second-guessing herself.

"Right," Colin confirmed. "Kate said she'd be here as soon as possible, by the way."

"We know it wasn't Max," Hannah said.

"And he would have been the first on the list of suspects, had he not been taken into custody," Colin agreed.

"He's probably the first person ever to be grateful he's in jail!" Hannah noted. Then she turned to the back door, it was still ajar. The warmth and the light seemed to beckon her in. "Why don't we wait in the house so you can warm up?" she offered Colin.

"I'm still not sure that's a good idea," he said.

Despite his protests, Hannah made her way to the back door and stepped inside the house.

"Hannah, wait!" he tried one last time.

Meanwhile, Hannah had walked into the home, preparing herself to snoop around. Before she could make her way too far past the entrance, she was almost run over by Stephanie, racing downstairs from her bedroom. She was frantic and out of breath. "What are you doing here?" she asked, surprised to see Hannah. "And where's Theodore?" she said between breaths. "I've been waiting for him in our bedroom."

Hannah stood between her and the door, attempting to block her from seeing her dead fiancé.

Stephanie could sense something was wrong and pushed her way past Hannah. She ran out into the backyard and by the pool where Colin was sitting beside a lifeless Theodore. "What? What's going on?" she kneeled beside Theodore and took his face in her hands. "Theodore! Wake up! Wake up!" Now she was gently tapping his face, hoping to rouse him from what she was desperate to believe was a deep sleep.

Colin placed a gentle hand on her shoulder. "Stephanie, I'm so sorry," he said.

At this, she began sobbing. She leaned over Theodore's body, her face close to his, tears falling onto his blue-tinted lips. She mourned the shock of her fiancé's death loudly. Mazie sat, watching the spectacle with a head slightly tilted to the left as if trying to understand what was going on.

Sensing she needed space, Colin slowly stepped away from her and pulled Hannah aside.

"Colin," Hannah spoke first. "Something feels off about this whole thing. Even if Stephanie was fast asleep, wouldn't she have heard us at the door? If not when I knocked, when I rang the doorbell?"

Colin looked from Hannah to Stephanie, as if trying to piece it all together.

As the two were discussing the situation, Kate Carver and Ralph rounded the side of the house. Ralph directed the paramedics to the already dead Theodore.

Kate stopped by Hannah and Colin to find out what had happened, exactly. They replayed the events as they experienced them, Hannah finding herself unable to keep her suspicions about Stephanie to herself. "Kate, it just seems too convenient for her to happen upon him after we'd been here for all this time," she said. "And why would the door have been wide open?"

Kate nodded and thanked Hannah and Colin. She walked toward Stephanie. "Stephanie, this is going to be very difficult for you, but I need to ask you some questions about this evening. If we are to find out what happened to Theodore, there is no time to wait."

Stephanie continued sobbing, wiping her nose with her sleeve. She began to hiccup and nodded. "Okay, how can I help?" she managed between gasps for breath. Kate had been questioning Stephanie for only a few minutes when Hannah and Colin heard her loud protests. "I'm innocent! How can you think I would ever do such a thing?" she shouted, her voice loud and clear now.

"These are just routine questions," Kate responded, hoping to calm Stephanie down. "Why don't you come with us to the station where we can do this in a more comfortable setting." She looked down at Theodore's body. "Maybe it would be nice to get away from the scene for a while."

Tears streamed down Stephanie's face once again. "I didn't do this!" she cried, as Kate led her to the patrol car.

CHAPTER EIGHT

*H*annah and Colin walked Mazie back to her place, but their night of investigation was far from over. After they settled Mazie with some food and water, they both turned right back to the door. "I'll drive?" she asked Colin, dangling her keys. "I'll follow," he replied.

They made their way to the police station. Kate hadn't expressly asked her to follow, but Hannah couldn't think of a better place to be to help get to the bottom of the case.

They situated themselves in the lobby, waiting for an opportunity to speak with Kate. When they saw her emerge from the back, Hannah jumped up. "Kate! How did it go questioning Stephanie?" she asked.

Kate waved. "Hi, Hannah! Why don't you both come back to my office for a minute, where we can chat in private?" she said in a lowered voice.

Hannah and Colin obediently followed her behind the counter of the police station. She sat behind her desk and they sat opposite. "Thank you so much for calling us tonight," she began.

Hannah and Colin nodded.

"To be honest, the case seems open and shut. As you know, Max was in custody here, so he couldn't have physically pulled it off. And no one else was near the house. Which means it had to be Stephanie."

Hannah listened carefully. All signs did point to Stephanie, but something about it still didn't sit right with her.

Kate continued. "We think that after she saw Max, Stephanie realized how much she missed him and decided to take matters into her own hands," she continued.

Colin nodded. "She wanted to have her cake and eat it too."

Hannah shook her head. "But how could she have her cake, if she didn't marry Theodore Murphy? She would have nothing to gain if she murdered him before marrying him," Hannah disagreed.

"Ah, that's where it gets interesting," Kate continued. "Nadine confirmed with us that Theodore had recently revised his will to include Stephanie. Effective immediately. So, were he to die before the marriage, she'd still get his fortune. It looks like Stephanie was an heiress and it gives her quite a motive." Kate's eyebrows went up as if to suggest there was no further reason to doubt Stephanie's guilt.

"Yikes," Colin said. "It will be hard to argue her way out of that one."

Hannah blew out the breath she'd been holding. "That is a tough fact to argue," she agreed. "And I guess that's why Nadine came to my office so bothered in the first place. She must have sensed something was off about the whole thing."

Kate confirmed with a nod. "Stephanie simply couldn't wait to get her hands on Theodore's fortune.

And seeing Max made her realize that there was no time to waste."

Hannah didn't know why something still felt off, but she could find no argument against the theory. "Thanks for seeing us, Kate. I supposed I can wrap up the investigation on my side of things." She stood up and slowly made her way to the door. "But it does make me curious as to why Nadine was so eager for me to stop investigating earlier today." She shrugged and walked out of the office.

She and Colin walked to the lobby area, where they saw both Nadine and Mrs. Lynch arrive at the police station. "I'm so sorry for your loss," she called. "What a night it's been." Then she looked at Nadine. "I wish we could have been there sooner. Maybe we could have helped save your father." She looked down at her feet.

Nadine reached out to grab Hannah and pulled her into an embrace. "Thank you so much, Hannah. If you hadn't been there tonight, who knows when we would have found out about my father, or what Stephanie may have done to cover her tracks. You were a huge help. I appreciate it." She smiled sadly.

"By the way, I'm sorry I didn't stop the investigation as you requested," she felt she had to add.

Nadine shook her head dismissively. "We wouldn't be here without you. Thank you for your persistence."

Hannah noted Nadine's genuine sadness about the loss of her father, and how Mrs. Lynch comforted her. She tried to push any lingering doubts out of the way. There seemed to be no room for any other theory. She looped her arm around Colin's and started toward the exit when she heard her name.

"Oh, Hannah?"

Hannah turned to see who was calling her.

"Hannah, would you mind stepping back here for a minute? There's something I'd like you to see," Ralph said from behind the counter. Kate's trusty deputy was calling her back. She wondered what it could be about.

"I'll wait here," Colin said, taking a seat in the lobby, offering his hand to take Mazie's leash.

She handed the leash over, nodded, and went to follow Ralph.

"Someone would like to speak with you," he said, leading her past Kate's office and toward the holding cells.

"Is Stephanie still trying to plead her innocence?" Hannah asked Ralph.

"Not exactly."

He took out his collection of keys and found the one to the men's holding cell. She glanced up at him, surprised. He ushered her in and stood her in front of Max. Max was standing behind the bars with a pleading look.

"How can I help you, Max?" she asked, extremely curious.

"Hannah. I've been able to piece together bits of what has gone on tonight from behind bars," he began. "I heard yelling through the walls and recognized it as Stephanie. I'm guessing she's a suspect?" he asked.

Hannah nodded to confirm.

"You need to hear me out," he begged.

"Go ahead, then," Hannah encouraged.

"Can you tell me why she was taken in?" he asked.

Hannah repeated the theory she had just discussed in Kate's office. "She was the only one on the scene. She claims that she is such a deep sleeper, she slept through it all. Even when Colin and I were ringing the doorbell she didn't wake up. That seems unlikely. And given the fact that Theodore had just changed his will to include her, without being married, we think she saw you and realized how much she missed you and decided to kill him so she could be with you and still have the money."

"You've got to understand, Stephanie is a very deep sleeper. And *I* should know," he added, conspiratorially. "That woman could sleep through a tsunami. I know it may sound like it, but what she's saying isn't crazy at all," he said, grabbing the bars now. "I'm just asking that you consider the possibility that Stephanie is innocent here. I've known her for a long time, and she is not a murderer." He locked eyes with Hannah.

Hannah studied him carefully. "Tell me, then. Who do you think could have done it?" she asked.

Max shrugged. "That I don't know. I just know it

wasn't her. It couldn't have been. She wouldn't hurt a fly. In fact, one time she actually stopped me from killing a fly just so she could release it outside," he said, his mind now far away in a memory.

"I'll consider the possibility, Max. But one thing does concern me."

"What's that?" he asked.

"Why should I believe you, when you could benefit from her being free after this? Once you get out, it would be pretty convenient for you to have a wealthy girlfriend to welcome you with open arms." She eyed him carefully.

"I'm the first to admit that I'd love a rich girlfriend," he agreed. "But that's not what this is about. There is no way Stephanie could have done this." He moved to the bench in the cell and dropped his head into his hands.

As she watched him Hannah felt that he was telling the truth. It was just a feeling but it felt right and she couldn't help but think that it was worth investigating. "I'll look into it, Max," she said to him.

He looked up and gave her a weary smile. "Thanks."

Hannah followed Ralph back out to the waiting area where Colin was looking at his phone. "Ready to head out now?" she asked.

Colin tucked the phone back into his pocket. "You bet." He held the door for her. Hannah looked back in the lobby to see Mrs. Lynch and Nadine, still sitting, waiting. Her eyes lingered on them for just a moment before she turned back to walk into the cold night air.

CHAPTER NINE

When Colin closed the car door behind him, and Hannah was sure they were alone with no one listening, she reported back what Max had said in the cell block. "He seemed really genuine, Colin."

"Most criminals do," he said, smiling at her. "Max could probably sell a car to a car salesman."

Hannah swatted his shoulder. "I know, I know he's a conman. But this feels like something more. Yes, he's a hothead, and he's a little slimy, but the way he came to Stephanie's defense felt surprisingly authentic to me," she argued.

"So, what are you going to do?" he asked.

"Why don't we offer to take Nadine and Mrs. Lynch back to their place?" she asked. "Then we can just keep an eye out for anything suspicious."

"Sounds good to me, I'll wait here while you get them," he said.

Hannah opened the car door and went back to poke her head into the police station. "Hi, ladies," she started. "I'm so sorry, but I didn't even think to offer you both a ride home. How rude of me! Would you like to hop in with us? We are driving right past the lake house."

Mrs. Lynch sighed in relief. "Thank you so much, we would love that. It's a little bit too cold and too dark for this old body to be navigating the icy sidewalks," she replied.

"Thanks, Hannah," Nadine added. "That would be fantastic."

Nadine and Mrs. Lynch hopped into the back seat of Hannah's car, with Colin at the wheel. Mazie was in the back seat, sitting between her new guests, trying to lick them, her tail wagging the whole time. "You'll have to excuse Mazie!" Hannah called back. "She loves new people."

Mrs. Lynch patted Mazie's head dismissively, while Nadine moved her purse away from the hound looking somewhat annoyed. Mazie tried walking on Nadine's lap to smell the contents, but she gently kept her at bay. "No, thanks, doggie."

"Mazie, leave it, sit," Hannah said from the front seat. Mazie sat obediently between the two ladies and looked adoringly at Hannah.

When Colin arrived at the lake house, he helped everyone out and to the house.

"Would you like to come in for some coffee?" Mrs. Lynch offered.

"Oh, I'd love some," Hannah replied, suddenly feeling a wave of exhaustion take her over.

"I'll wait in the car, I have some calls to make," Colin said. "I'll just keep it warm for when you are ready to head home," he said to Hannah.

When Mrs. Lynch, Hannah, and Nadine were all inside, Mrs. Lynch busied herself with brewing a fresh pot of coffee. Nadine slumped onto a kitchen stool. "I just can't believe this happened," she said rubbing at her eyes. "I wish I had come to you sooner." A single tear dropped down her cheek.

"Now, listen here, Nadine," Mrs. Lynch piped in. "Women like Stephanie will always pull the wool over a man's eyes. It's not his fault, and it's certainly not yours. There is only one person to blame, and that is Stephanie. And I know it doesn't take away the pain, but we can at least be confident that she's well on her way to paying for her crime and that she will go away for a long time. She will never hurt anyone again."

Hannah watched as Nadine seemed comforted by Mrs. Lynch's words. Mrs. Lynch set three mugs in front of them and poured them each a hot cup.

After taking a sip, Nadine groaned. "I'm starving!" and opened her purse to take out a change purse. But instead of coins, she poured a handful of pecan clusters into the palm of her hand.

"Ah, that's what Mazie was so interested in," Hannah said out loud. Just then, Mazie put her front paws on Nadine's legs as if to ask for a nibble.

Nadine shrugged the dog away. "This is just the treat

I need to calm my nerves, thank you, Mrs. Lynch," she said, just before popping them into her mouth.

Hannah got the impression that the pecan clusters were more than just a handful of nuts, but she wasn't one to judge and looked away.

Mazie, on the other hand, was in full judgment that Nadine had rebuffed her request for a treat, and pulled mightily on her leash, all but yanking Hannah from her seat. Then Mazie turned and walked to the back door. Startled, Hannah jumped off her stool to follow the beagle. "My apologies, ladies. It looks as though Mazie needs a little break outside," she said, following her dog to the door.

Just as soon as Mazie was outside, she yanked herself free from Hannah, running to a spot behind a potted plant in the backyard. "Mazie, no!" Hannah scolded, running after her dog. When she finally caught up, she saw Mazie sniffing a cluster of similar pecan treats, spilled behind on the ground behind the plant. She quickly intercepted Mazie but the beagle wasn't after eating them. She had found a clue. "Mazie!" she said in a pleased voice.

Nadine came rushing out behind her. "Is everything

okay out here?" she asked. "I heard yelling." She jogged over to where Hannah and Mazie were standing. Hannah gave her a hard look, and Nadine froze, lowering her eyes to the area Mazie had been sniffing. Her face grew pale as she realized what the dog had just found.

Hannah, now in full control of Mazie's leash, crossed her arms in front of her chest. "Do you have anything to say for yourself?" Hannah asked.

Nadine shook her head feebly. Hannah watched as she tried to form words that wouldn't come out of her dry mouth.

"Let me fill in the blanks for you," Hannah said. "I think you used those pecans to drug your father, hoping that nature would take a deadly course." She stared hard at Nadine who remained shocked and speechless, staring at the pecans. "And when nature did exactly as you intended, you conveniently placed the blame on Stephanie."

Nadine finally found her voice, just as Mrs. Lynch came rushing out of the house to join them. "No! That's not at all what happened!" Nadine protested. "Nothing could be further from the truth. Don't you remember that I came to you in the first place? Why would I have wanted to hire you if I had just planned to kill my dad in the end? I wouldn't want anyone investigating that!" she cried.

Hannah had to admit she had a point, but something was off. "The timing of all of this felt a little bit too convenient," she said. Then she took out her phone. "I'm going to call Kate and Ralph to come over again. Maybe they can help solve this problem," she said.

At this, Nadine panicked. "No, stop!" she yelled. "I only tried the treats because Mrs. Lynch suggested them. Isn't that right?" she turned to the older woman for confirmation.

Mrs. Lynch looked at them both as if evaluating the situation.

"Isn't that right, Mrs. Lynch?" Nadine tried again. "I just learned about these pecan treats. I wouldn't have had time to drug my father with them. I also wouldn't know where to get enough of them to do so," she said.

Hannah turned her eyes to the housekeeper, who was staring back at her. The look she gave was cold and emotionless.

CHAPTER TEN

Mrs. Lynch remained still and said nothing.

Hannah looked between the two women, her mind connecting the dots. "Mrs. Lynch, might it be possible that you were the one who began planting the seeds of doubt in Nadine's mind?"

Mrs. Lynch pursed her lips. "And what exactly do you mean by that, Hannah?"

Hannah looked to the other woman. "Nadine, when you first met Stephanie, what was your impression of her?"

Nadine thought for a moment. "I obviously thought

she was quite young, but otherwise, she seemed rather sweet," she replied.

"I see. And at what point did you begin to wonder about her?"

Nadine looked contemplative.

"To put it another way, why did you come to my office to see if I could help?" she pushed.

Nadine looked nervously at Mrs. Lynch. "Now I come to think of it, it was after I had afternoon tea at my father's house with Mrs. Lynch. She started asking questions about Stephanie that made me feel suspicious about her motives," she replied.

"It is my job as a staff member of the lake home to be on the watch for the best interest of everyone. Whether that is serving tea to a guest, or ensuring Theodore is being cared for," she folded her arms across her chest.

Nadine looked back at Hannah. "She's right – and I'm appreciative of it!" she added. "I'm not around my father that much..." her voice wobbled for a minute and she bit back a tear, "or, I wasn't around my father as much as I should have been," she corrected, looking at the ground. "Not nearly as often as I used to be. So, I rely on Mrs. Lynch to keep me informed of his whereabouts, his health, and anything else I might need to be aware of," Nadine said.

Mrs. Lynch lifted her chin triumphantly.

Hannah nodded, waiting for Nadine to finish. "Might I offer an alternative point of view?" she asked. Neither woman responded, so she continued. "Perhaps, Mrs. Lynch, you wanted Nadine to act out in some way, hence the treats. You thought by giving her the drugged pecans, she would behave poorly."

Mrs. Lynch shook her head furiously. "That is preposterous."

"Drugged!" Nadine said and stared hard at Mrs. Lynch.

Hannah continued her theory. "When Nadine didn't actually do what you needed, you saw that other eyes were on the household. Stephanie's eyes, to be exact."

"Where is this all leading, Hannah? It sounds to me that you are speaking gibberish," Mrs. Lynch said.

"You turned your attention from Nadine to Stephanie, and thought of a plan to frame her instead."

Nadine's eyes sparkled at this. Up until this moment, she hadn't been exactly sure what Hannah was insinuating with her line of questioning.

"When Max burst into the house this afternoon, you seized your opportunity," Hannah said.

Mrs. Lynch was chuckling under her breath now. "If nothing else, Hannah, you have a wild imagination." She looked over to Nadine and rolled her eyes as if trying to keep her on her side. "What does Max have to do with this, anyway. We all know he was behind bars when it happened."

"You used Max's jealous appearance to put more doubt in everyone's mind about Stephanie. You knew she slept hard, and you took advantage of her sleep patterns to set her up, and then," she paused for the moment to sink in, "you drugged Theodore. Making it look like Stephanie killed him."

Mrs. Lynch didn't move a muscle.

Nadine was listening carefully, processing all of the

details. "You know, Mrs. Lynch, my dad was always quite the ladies' man. Old, young, it didn't matter. There was always a woman on his arm. Why exactly were you so concerned with Stephanie?" she asked the older woman.

Mrs. Lynch's face pinched in what looked to be pain. "Stephanie was different," she spat.

"Now that I'm thinking about it, Mrs. Lynch, you were strangely adamant about your distrust of Stephanie. I wouldn't have thought twice about any of it had you not been so insistent. I really only grew concerned about her after you started dribbling all of that poison in my ear. And now I realize you were dribbling poison down my throat at the same time!" Nadine's posture had changed, she was fully alert, looking at Mrs. Lynch.

Mrs. Lynch had hardly blinked the whole time. Her eyes were glassy and there was a tick in her jaw. Like a cornered bear, she was carefully watching the two women in front of her.

Nadine pushed further. "Why did you do it, Mrs. Lynch?"

Without warning, a knife appeared in Mrs. Lynch's

hand. It was an 8-inch kitchen knife and must have come from her pocket. As she held it in front of her, it glinted under the landscape lights.

Nadine gasped and lurched away from the knife. "I don't understand this, all the time you spent with him... why were you so upset about my father's money?" she asked almost sobbing once more.

Mrs. Lynch waved the knife between Nadine and Hannah, stepping forward and back as if deciding her next move. "It was never about the money," she said in a low growl. Then she lifted the knife higher and held it firmly in the air between them. Her voice rose an octave as she gathered her courage. "It was about the fact that Theodore was ready to marry again," she was shaking now, her eyes flashed with anger.

Nadine's eyebrows squished together. "Mrs. Lynch, I don't understand."

Mrs. Lynch's voice was now in a screech. "Theodore was ready to marry again, and he was not going to marry *me*!" she cried.

CHAPTER ELEVEN

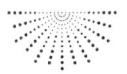

Hannah knew she had to do something if they were to get out of this alive. Her jaw dropped in shock as Mrs. Lynch admitted to murdering Theodore! "You killed Theodore, the man you say you loved because you were jealous of Stephanie?"

Mrs. Lynch snarled and lurched at Hannah, but she stepped back and the blade caught nothing but air.

"I've always loved Theodore," she growled. "I've been waiting for him to realize that he loved me in return. His engagement to Stephanie helped me realize that it was never going to happen... I couldn't bear it any longer," she admitted.

"So, you killed him by way of revenge?" Hannah clarified.

Mrs. Lynch nodded, still gripping her knife.

Hannah cast a quick glance over to Nadine, who was standing, eyes wide.

"I hope it was all worth it because you are going to pay for your crime!" Hannah said.

Mrs. Lynch laughed maniacally, inching closer to Nadine with her knife. "How adorable that you think I'm going to pay for anything. I will get away with this, just as long as there are no witnesses," she trained her eyes on Nadine.

Nadine's eyes widened with fear as she watched Mrs. Lynch come closer.

With a lurch, Mrs. Lynch stabbed the knife in Nadine's direction and slashed her cheek. Nadine screamed and put her hand to her face. Blood ran between her fingers. When she took it away, there was thick, red blood on her hand.

Hannah watched the scene in horror, realizing Mrs. Lynch was now heading toward her. Mazie had been sitting beside Hannah until this moment. Sensing danger for her owner, she jumped in to intervene on behalf of Hannah. Mazie lurched toward Mrs. Lynch with one jump, sinking her teeth into her ankle.

Mrs. Lynch cried out in pain and before she could reach down to push the beagle away, she overbalanced and fell face first. The knife tumbled out of her hand as she landed with a thump on the wet grass. Mazie had her jaws gripped tightly around Mrs. Lynch's ankle and was not letting go. Hannah stepped carefully toward Mrs. Lynch and kicked the end of the knife until it skittered away from her and stopped just before the pool. Its heavy silver blade shone beneath the lights and seemed to warn of pain to come. Hannah shuddered but turned her attention back to the woman on the ground.

There was nothing to worry about. Whenever Mrs. Lynch tried to move, Mazie was there, growling and tightening her grip on the woman's ankle. "Okay, okay, I'll be still!" she cried.

Hannah checked her phone. "They should be here any minute, Nadine. Hang in there."

Nadine was ghost-white at this point, her face still

bleeding, and combined with the shock of discovering who had murdered her father she looked like a woman lost.

The sound of a patrol car's siren announced the arrival of Kate and Ralph, blocks before they came running into the back yard. Colin was following close behind them. Ralph ran directly to Mrs. Lynch and placed her in cuffs. He and Kate hoisted her to her feet. "Do you have anything to say for yourself, Mrs. Lynch?" Kate asked.

"Oh, do I!" she yelled. "I had every right to kill Theodore. I was saving him from himself! I was saving him from another money-grubbing lover!" Kate nodded to Ralph, indicating it was time to take her into custody.

As she walked away, Nadine gathered her senses and shouted back to her. "You didn't save him from anything! You selfish woman, you were only focused on yourself!" When the woman didn't turn to look at Nadine, she continued, "You killed him!" Then she turned to face Hannah. "How can I ever thank you?" she walked toward Hannah and grabbed her arm.

"Well, to begin with, let's get that nasty gash taken care of, and then maybe we can clean you up a bit," Hannah replied, gently shifting her arm away from Nadine.

Nadine nodded and then seemed to spot the blood on her hand. She grimaced at the mess she'd left on Hannah's shirt. "Oh, no, I am so sorry!" she said. "I can't believe I just did that!"

Hannah smiled. "It's a shirt, don't worry about it."

Kate put her arm around Nadine. "Let's get you inside, we can warm you up, get you cleaned up and the paramedics can take a look at your face," she said.

Hannah watched and felt Colin put his arm around her. She had the urge to lean back and just stay there forever. Instead, she turned and gave him her thanks with a nod, then she looked for Mazie.

The little beagle sat in front of the knife. She only moved when one of the crime scene techs bagged it. With that, she ran back and Hannah scooped her into her arms and pulled her close. "You saved me, you little hero," she said as she rained kisses down on the beagle's head.

Mazie snuffled into her cheek returning her kisses all the while wagging her tail against Hannah's side.

Colin put his arm around her again. "You're freezing," he said, rubbing her arm to warm her up. "Hey," he said quietly to Hannah.

She looked up at him. "Yes?"

"You okay?" he asked. "That sounded like quite the ordeal. I'm sorry I didn't come to check on you before. I figured you were warm and cozy inside, drinking coffee, and talking about Max." He looked at her apologetically.

She moved her body closer to his. "I'm better than okay." She looked up to meet his gaze. "I just cracked the case!" She tried to keep the excitement out of her voice. Given the situation, it wouldn't have been altogether appropriate, but she was feeling very proud of herself.

Colin grinned, his eyes sparkling. He squeezed her tight and kissed the top of her head. "Nice work, Hannah, and nice work, Mazie." With that, he kissed the beagle's head too.

CHAPTER TWELVE

"Kate, hi!" Hannah said, answering the front door of her home to find Kate Carver standing there.

"Hi, Hannah, I was hoping you and Mazie would like to go on a walk with me. There's a lot for us to catch up on!" she said.

Mazie was at the door, tail flying wildly back and forth having heard the word "walk". Hannah smiled down at her puppy. "There's no way back now!" She clipped on Mazie's harness and they filed out the door.

"Anything new with the case?" Hannah asked.

"No new developments, but we have officially indicted Mrs. Lynch on the murder of Theodore Murphy," she replied.

"Oh, that's fantastic news!" Hannah said.

"We also released Stephanie and Max," she added.

Hannah raised her eyebrows at Kate. "Together?" she asked suggestively.

Kate chuckled. "Stephanie was released first, but she did wait in the lobby until Max was out." She turned to smile at Hannah. "And yes, they did leave the precinct together."

Hannah smiled. "I'll check in on Stephanie. I'd like to hear about her experience now that we know she's innocent. I hope she's holding up okay," Hannah called over the noise of a loud engine.

Kate pointed to a Harley with two people on it pulling toward them. It swung over to the curb and parked on the street. "Looks like you won't have to wait for long to find out," she said.

The woman removed her arms from the waist of the man in front of her. Stepping off the bike they removed their helmets, revealing that they were

Stephanie and Max, as Kate had hinted. "Hannah!" Stephanie said, stepping toward them.

"Oh, Chief... Mrs. Carver," Stephanie said, stepping closer to Max. "I didn't realize it was you."

Kate gave her a friendly smile. "Don't worry, Stephanie, you are fully in the clear now. You have nothing to be scared of."

Stephanie nodded. "Yes, sorry. Just seeing you brings back bad memories from being behind bars," she said, twirling her hair on her index finger.

"Believe it or not, I get that a lot," Kate replied. She stepped back a few feet to make Stephanie feel more comfortable.

"So, how are you two doing?" Hannah asked. "Are you a ..." she looked between the two of them, noting their flushed cheeks, wondering if it was the cold winter air or love. "Are you two together again?" she came right out and asked it.

Max wrapped his tattooed arm around Stephanie and pulled her close. She turned her face to look at his, and he gazed adoringly down at her. Then he placed a hand on her cheek and brought her in for a gentle kiss. When they were finished with their display of affection, they turned back to Hannah and Kate. "We are together again," Max confirmed.

Stephanie snuggled into his side. "I couldn't have seen it coming if you had paid me." Then she looked surprised at her own words and added quickly, "Not that I am being paid, or ever was, or even wanted to be!" She looked at Kate, concerned she might be locked right back up if she wasn't careful.

"Stephanie, I know it was a turn of phrase. We have a very guilty Mrs. Lynch behind bars, trust me, you can relax!" Kate said.

Stephanie's shoulders relaxed slightly. "Well, I didn't see it coming. That's for sure. But in jail, we could sort of communicate between the wall, and I started to feel the old feelings," she smiled up at him. "Then when we were released, I found out he was the one that came to my defense with you, Hannah. And if he hadn't done that, Mrs. Lynch might still be free!"

"That's true," Hannah said.

"Max was always my number one cheerleader when we were together. And being behind bars seems to have changed him a little bit," she put her hand on his chest. "He seems, I don't know, softer somehow."

Max studied the grass at Hannah's feet very carefully, a blush dangerously close to creeping up from under his collar. "We made a vow to start again, start fresh," he managed to say without making eye contact.

"That we did," Stephanie beamed. Anyway, we just wanted to thank you, Hannah. We owe you, big time!" she said.

"It's genuinely my pleasure," she replied. "I'm just happy that the real criminal is behind bars now."

Stephanie and Max waved goodbye to the ladies, hopping back on Max's Harley. Hannah and Kate watched them ride away.

"That's got to feel good," Kate said to Hannah.

"Oh, that feels amazing," she replied. "An unexpected bonus to being a P.I., that's for sure."

Kate and Hannah were back at her place now. "Thanks for stopping by, and catching me up on everything," Hannah said. "I'm sure I'll be seeing more of you as time goes on!"

Kate winked at her. "I'm sure you will, just remember to stay safe!" she replied.

When Hannah and Mazie were back in her house, settling into the couch together with a book in hand, Hannah's phone rang.

Hannah didn't recognize the number on the caller I.D. "Hello?" she answered.

It was Nadine.

"Oh, sure. I'd love to meet you there. I'll be right over," she replied. Nadine wanted to officially settle her business with Hannah as her P.I., and she wanted to do it at Hannah's office.

Hannah and Mazie hopped into her car and made their way over. The office space was no more organized since they last met there. Hannah had been too occupied solving the case to spend time filing papers and opening boxes.

Nadine was out front, waiting.

"Come on in," Hannah said, unlocking the office. She flicked the light switch to on and the single light bulb flickered, threatening not to glow for them.

Hannah directed Nadine to the same old couch and she sat across from her. "How are things?" Hannah asked.

Nadine reached into her purse, pulling out a stack of papers. "Things are," she paused and looked at Hannah, "good. All things considered. Now that the dust has settled slightly, I'm working through the paperwork for the estate."

Hannah nodded sympathetically. It had to be a difficult process, given all she had recently been through.

"Stephanie was indeed included in my father's will. He recently modified it. I considered going to a lawyer to fight it, but then remembered our conversation with Mrs. Lynch." She shuffled the papers slightly. "Stephanie's not a bad girl. I think she genuinely cared for my dad and she made him happy. I think if they had married, she seems like she would have been faithful."

Hannah smiled.

"And, love knows no age, am I right?" she let out a short laugh. "And I think it's fair to say Mrs. Lynch was manipulating the whole thing with her jealousy. So, Stephanie will get her inheritance."

"That must have been a hard decision to make, but it sounds like you are at peace," Hannah replied.

"I am. And there's another thing I'm happy about," Nadine said, lifting an envelope.

Hannah raised her eyebrows. "Oh?"

"Here you go," she handed it to Hannah.

Hannah peeked in the envelope and pulled out a check. "Oh!" she exclaimed. "That was kind of you." Then she studied the amount on the check and dropped the envelope in shock. "OH!" she exclaimed again, louder this time. "That was VERY kind of you," she looked at Nadine. "I don't really know what to say. This is such a generous amount." She looked between Nadine and the check.

Nadine smiled. "If it weren't for you, I would be eating pecans, and be manipulated by Mrs. Lynch, as we speak. Not to mention the fact that Stephanie would be wrongly jailed for the murder of my father. This is honestly the least I could do. I'm just so appreciative," she said, clasping her hands around

Hannah's. Then she joked, "And look, I even washed my hands before touching you this time!"

Hannah laughed. "Oh, Nadine. I'm so sorry about your father, but I'm so glad I was able to help provide some closure for you. Thank you so much for this," she held up the check. "I don't know what to say."

Nadine glanced around the office space. "Maybe you could use some of it to spruce this place up?" she grinned.

Hannah followed her eye line to the dusty boxes strewn about and chucked. "Maybe I will."

CHAPTER THIRTEEN

When Nadine left her office, Hannah looked around and felt a new burst of inspiration. She put the check in the small safe beneath her desk she had invested in and got to work. She moved boxes, unpacked them, organized the furniture, and even filed some papers. Mazie followed faithfully behind her, wherever she went.

She was deep in focus when she heard the chimes on the front door ring, indicating someone had come in.

She turned to see who it was. "Colin!" She went over to give him a hug.

He squeezed her tight, and then pulled her away to look at her. "Looks like you've been busy," he laughed, using his thumb to wipe some dirt off of her cheek.

She felt her skin warm under his touch and tilted her head. "I guess I'm finally making this place look respectable like a real P.I. might work here," she winked at him.

"I said I was sorry about that!" Colin said, referencing their last conversation in the office space. "Will you please forgive me?"

She waved his words away. "Already forgiven, I was just kidding around," she said. "But, listen. Nadine Murphy just came by and gave me a very large check for my services," she gave Colin a sly grin. "What do you say we celebrate somewhere special?"

Colin's eyebrows raised suggestively. "Somewhere like...?"

She moved to put her hand on his chest. "I don't know, maybe... Troughton's Trough?" she waited to hear his response, eyes shining.

He smiled down at her, putting his hand over hers. "I thought you'd never ask."

Hannah looked at her watch. "Why don't I get

cleaned up a little bit," she suggested. "Then Mazie and I will be over in about, oh, half an hour?"

Colin's smile filled the room. "I'll be counting the minutes." He brought his lips to her cheek and gave her a lingering kiss, then locked eyes with her before leaving.

Hannah waved her hand at her face willing her body temperature to lower. "Same here," she whispered.

Exactly thirty minutes later, she and Mazie were sitting on the terrace of his restaurant, enjoying the heat lamps and snuggled up under the lap blankets the restaurant provided. "To you, Hannah," he said, raising a glass to her.

She lifted hers in response.

"To a job well done!" he announced.

She met his glass with hers, and they sipped to her success.

As they put their glasses on the table, Oscar and Anita Gomez turned the corner, heading toward them.

Hannah brightened to see her friends, despite them having left on awkward terms the last time they spoke. She was still buoyed from her meeting with Nadine.

Oscar and Anita stopped in front of Hannah's table and stood nervously. "We heard about your great work on the Murphy murder," Oscar said. "Congratulations. You must be thrilled."

Anita smiled. "It's a good thing you didn't listen to us then, right?" she raised her eyebrows, at Hannah, waiting for her to admonish them.

Instead, Hannah stood and wrapped them both in a hug. "Thank you both. It was sweet of you to say so. And all is forgiven between us," she added.

She heard Anita sigh. "Oh, Hannah. I'm so relieved to hear that! We've missed you so much."

"We have missed you so much, and we really are sorry," Oscar added.

"Why don't you two come join us?" Colin asked, standing to add two chairs to their table. "There's lots of room. I'm sure Hannah would love to give you the details of the case!" he said.

"Are you sure? We won't be interrupting?" Anita asked.

"Not at all," Hannah said. "We'd love to have you, come on over!"

Anita and Oscar gratefully joined the couple. Mazie was quick to come over and greet them as well. "Ah, Mazie!" Oscar said rubbing her between the ears. "We have missed you – maybe the most!" he cast a teasing glance at Hannah as he said it. Mazie happily wagged her tail and savored Oscar's ear scratches.

When everyone had their food, and Mazie had been tossed enough scraps to be satisfied for a week, the four of them settled into easy conversation. Hannah couldn't help but feel that there was more going on with the Gómezes, but she wasn't sure how to approach it.

Mazie, on the other hand, had no qualms about it. She was pawing at both Oscar and Anita's legs, long after the food was gone.

"What's going on down there, Mazie?" Hannah asked. "There's no more food, leave the poor Gómezes alone!" But Mazie didn't understand, and she kept at it.

Hannah looked from her puppy to the couple. "Is everything all right with you both?" she asked.

She watched as Anita and Oscar exchanged a quick glance. Then Anita's hand moved over to Oscar's back as if to comfort him.

"Guys?" she asked. "Is there something you want to tell me?" Hannah was getting nervous now.

"Hannah, we actually have something we want to ask you," Oscar began.

"And we want you to know that our apologies are sincere. We hope it doesn't feel opportunistic, us coming to you this way," Anita added.

"All right, you two. You're making my heart rate go up. What exactly is it?" Hannah prodded.

"We think we need some of your help," Anita said.

"Some of your P.I. help," Oscar added.

"With one of our former employees," Anita finished.

Mazie had finally stopped pawing the couple, and Hannah reached down to scoop her up into her lap. She looked over at Colin, searching his face for something. She didn't know what; advice? Comfort?

He shrugged as if to communicate that it was her decision alone.

Hannah turned back to the couple and broke the silence. "What can I do to help?"

∽

If you enjoyed this book Grab Smudge and the Stolen Puppies FREE when you join my newsletter here

Read on for 2 amazing boxsets

CUPCAKES AND CRIMES BOOKS 1 TO 6 PREVIEW

Ding. Melody stretched the dough a little further; holding her breath as she expertly pulled it just enough to ensure a perfectly thin, translucent layer. The bell pinged again, and Melody glanced around for Kerry.

"Hey, Ker—where are you?" she called, failing to detect her assistant's presence. Melody shook her head, wiped her hands on her apron, exited the kitchen and hurried into the shop. There stood her best customer, Alvin Hennessy, the small town's local sheriff, his kind brown eyes lighting up as Melody came into his view. He hastily removed his hat, cleared his throat and smiled sheepishly down at her.

"Oh, hey there, Mel. Sorry to stop in again today, but I forgot I needed a cake for Ma's hen party tonight." Alvin shuffled his feet shyly, his cheeks reddening.

Melody sighed. She was grateful for his business, but suspected he purposely cut his order in two so he had an excuse to drop by twice today. She would have preferred efficiency, but good manners and a genuine fondness for the sheriff prevented her from showing any exasperation. She should be flattered by his attention—she knew, but she really wasn't interested in a romantic relationship at this point in her life. Not that he wasn't handsome, in his own way, but he was just not her type, she supposed, even if she *were* in the market for a romantic relationship. She took a quick moment to evaluate his appearance. He possessed the long, lean lines of a thoroughbred, but somehow wasn't able to project his inherent attractiveness, even in uniform. Perhaps it was his constant grinning. It made him appear a little strange, no, that wasn't really it; it was more his inability to realize his own appeal, a slight insecurity, an awkwardness. She mentally shook herself and focused on the business at hand.

"Not a problem, Al. Always good to see you!" she said, forcing a smile.

She felt a pang of guilt at her fib, but knew she probably made his day with her comment. In spite of her uncanny ability to notice and discern the overt as well as hidden attributes of others, Melody possessed a baffling blindness to her own qualities. She could have easily graced the pages of any magazine, even in jeans and her trademark logoed tee. An Irish beauty, Melody was blessed with more than her fair share of pluses: glossy auburn, shoulder-length tresses (albeit piled on her head and anchored with a hairnet), an angelic face, and statuesque curves to rival any pin-up girl. She had many secret (and not so secret) male admirers in town, but even though she was consistently friendly and courteous, she possessed an intimidating blend of self-assurance, the formerly discussed unawareness of her beauty, and a steadfast personal rule against flirting.

"What kind of cake did you have in mind? We have a cream cheese-filled red velvet and an orange-hickory nut on hand. Kerry made them yesterday, and they're still fresh."

As if summoned by her name, Kerry rushed in, flinging out hyper apologies as she whipped on an apron over her uniform of sparkly blue jeans and the shop's logo-emblazoned t-shirt.

"Where were you?" Melody asked.

"I forgot my phone in my car and wanted to make sure Aunt Rita didn't call with her family reunion order. I told her to call the shop rather than my cell, but she never remembers the number and can't be bothered to look it up. Good thing I checked; as she did leave me a voicemail with what she wants, and she's hoping to get everything tomorrow afternoon, even though the reunion doesn't start until Friday evening!" Kerry's words tumbled over each other as her hands gestured wildly. Melody wondered how Kerry was able to breathe while talking at such a rate.

"I see you've gone over your quota of caffeine today," Melody teased, noting Kerry's messy blond bun slipping out of the hair net stretched crookedly over her head and the slight sheen of sweat on her brow.

Kerry, plump and pretty, was engaged to Port Warren High's beloved football coach, George Stanley, who adored her. In Kerry's mind, this gave her free reign to play matchmaker with all her unfortunately single friends and acquaintances, especially her beautiful boss.

"Yeah, might have overdone the go-juice just a tad." Kerry chuckled, tucking her stray blond strands back into the net. Kerry then turned her attention to their visitor. "Hey, Al, you forget something? Weren't you in earlier?"

Alvin blushed and nodded, looking down at his shoes and rubbing his close-cropped brown hair.

Kerry smiled wickedly at his obvious discomfiture. "I'm beginning to think this is your new office!"

Melody gave her a quick, pursed-lip glare, knowing it would only encourage her would-be marriage broker to continue to tease poor Alvin.

"Yep, completely forgot about Ma's card deal tonight; she wanted me to pick up a cake; whatcha got in stock?" Alvin asked trying to recover himself.

As the sheriff switched his embarrassed attention to his torturer, Melody took the opportunity to slip quietly back into the kitchen to finish the croissants, leaving Kerry to fill Alvin's order. She concentrated, cutting and folding thin strips into perfect crescents.

"That guy's got it bad!" Kerry announced as she sailed into the kitchen, automatically beelining it for the coffee machine.

"No! You're cut off!" Melody was quick to see her assistant's intention and she grabbed Kerry's sleeve with a floury hand, "No more coffee for you!"

Kerry sheepishly set the pot back down and crossed her arms. She eyed the tray of bakery rejects that failed Melody's perfectionistic eye, sighed, and helped herself to a broken cookie. Nibbling, she glared at Melody.

"You've got it bad," Melody insisted. "You're torturing that poor man, and you know it! What did he end up buying?"

"Don't try and change the subject! That dog is one whipped puppy. If he really forgot that cake this morning, I'm a one-eyed frog. His mom has bridge every Wednesday night, tonight is no exception!" Kerry exclaimed while munching through a second cookie reject.

Melody shrugged, not wanting to encourage that line of thinking. She'd known for a while that Alvin had a thing for her. She tried her best to ignore it and avoid him as much as possible. With her busy schedule, she just wasn't ready for anything serious, even if it was with someone like Alvin. Or was it really about her schedule? Whatever, she was just not into a relationship at the moment. She had to admit, he was a good guy. And he would probably treat her right if she ever gave him a chance. But it was just too soon.

"He's either going to have to man up and ask you out or go broke buying donuts and cakes! For a lawman, he ain't very brave!" Kerry added.

Melody let her rattle on, hoping Kerry would run out of words on the subject, though that seemed unlikely.

Kerry propped her chin on her left palm looking all dreamy. "I think he's cute, though, don't you? A little on the puppy dog side, but still pretty manly when he's not tripping over his tongue when you're around."

Melody sighed, rolled her eyes, and kept silent. It was her weapon of choice and it worked well with Kerry, whose main hobby was verbalizing, combined with taking off on frequent, caffeine-infused rabbit trails. So, Kerry prattled on while Mel took a moment to mull over the situation.

In truth, she almost wished she reciprocated Alvin's apparent feelings. She dreaded the day she would really have to reject such a nice guy. She blew out a breath of frustration, hoping against hope that he would never find the courage to approach her romantically because in that way she could avoid the whole ordeal. If he did ever find the courage to ask her out, she would just have to find a nice way to turn him down. Maybe she should start thinking about how she could get out of it without hurting his feelings.

Her thoughts, generally practical, quickly switched over to Aunt Rita's reunion and she broke into Kerry's monologue.

"Which cake did the sheriff end up buying? And what does Aunt Rita need by Friday?" Melody asked and Kerry cooperated with the subject change, her talking talent showcased by her ability to jump off and on any topic train.

"He decided on the red velvet. Auntie said she needs three cakes: one devil's food, one pineapple upside down, and one hummingbird. I think I should call her and steer her away from the hummingbird, as it's too similar to the pineapple upside-down—don't you think? Maybe a pecan Texas sheet instead? Add a little variety? Also, she wants two-dozen each of chocolate chip, shortbread and peanut butter cookies, an apple strudel and six dozen dinner rolls. I think I better tell her to freeze everything when she gets it tomorrow since she's not serving most of it until Saturday and Sunday, and I wouldn't think she'd like them anything but fresh. Really, she should get everything from us Friday afternoon; we could have it done by two, don't you think? Maybe I should call her? Maybe not, as she never changes her mind once she makes a plan; maybe you should call her? She'd probably listen to you better than me. But maybe freezing them would be good enough and then we wouldn't be as stressed on Saturday, as we have that wedding cake to deliver and set up, and Jeannette isn't somebody we want to disappoint with shoddy work..." Kerry continued to ponder the quandary of her aunt's order while she bustled about wiping counters, putting away clean tools from the dish drainer, and checking—and double-checking—the stores of supplies.

Just then the bell dinged, heralding another customer, and Kerry whisked out of the kitchen.

Melody opened the oven and placed the croissant trays inside, setting the timer as she finished. She could hear Kerry's voice, presumably talking to a customer, and while tempted to start on tomorrow's orders, she knew she should make an appearance in the shop as some of her customers took it very personally when she was too busy to greet them.

Kerry's Aunt Rita stood at the counter, her lips pursed as she listened to her niece's flood of advice. Rita held up her hand, finally getting Kerry to slow her word flow. Aunt Rita had a closet full of old-fashioned, 50's style dresses that belted at the waist, everything from floral, to stripes and plaids, to plain. She only ever wore dark brown, laced up walking shoes, white gloves, and netted hats whenever she ventured outside her house. Inside, she wore button-up housedresses, ones she deemed suitable for the constant cleaning she inflicted on her house. Dust was terrified to land anywhere in her vicinity.

"I need everything by tomorrow afternoon, Kerry Ann, is that going to be a problem?" Just as Kerry opened her mouth to answer, Rita caught sight of Melody.

"Thank God you're here! My niece seems to think I don't know my own mind, and I need her to understand that I need everything tomorrow afternoon. I will be extremely busy with other reunion tasks... of course, I have to do everything myself, the rest of the family cannot be trusted... so I need the desserts squared away tomorrow. Is that too difficult?" Rita glared at Melody belligerently.

"Oh no, Rita, tomorrow afternoon is perfect! We don't have another big order besides yours due until Friday afternoon, so it will work out just fine, and your choices show nice forethought and variety," Melody assured her.

"Hmph. Kerry Ann here seems to think I don't have enough variety in the cake department. I keep trying to explain that Cousin Harold loves the pineapple upside down and my sister must have hummingbird. There is no room for substitutes. Now, I need to know if those choices are going to be a problem? I don't want to take my business elsewhere, but my friend Alice's cousin bakes and sells cakes out of her kitchen, so I do have other options," Rita continued to scowl pugnaciously at her niece while she directed her question to Melody.

"No, we can certainly bake all your choices," Melody replied calmly. "All your selections are just fine, and there is no finer cake baker than your niece here!"

Mollified, Kerry let go of her need to adjust Aunt Rita's cake menu, and smiled at her employer, "Awww shucks, boss-lady! You're the best!"

"Hmph," Rita grunted, clutching her giant purse more firmly to her chest, as if perhaps Melody and Kerry weren't to be trusted; she then adjusted her old-fashioned hat and exited with, "Okay then. I'll expect your delivery tomorrow afternoon, but no earlier than two pm, as I'll need an afternoon rest with all this working myself to death. And for what? Some ungrateful relatives who don't mind reaping the benefits of all my back-breaking labor!"

Kerry groaned, shaking her head. As soon as her aunt was out of earshot, she commented, "Oh my God, Aunt Rita is something else, isn't she? No wonder Uncle Leroy left this earth... her sunny disposition probably poisoned him to death!"

Melody smiled, suspecting Kerry probably inherited

her aunt's opinionated personality, and ability to talk at lightspeed. Though Kerry was liberally tempered with cheerfulness, Rita lacked pretty much any positive modifying trait.

Grab Cupcakes and Crimes books 1 to 6 here

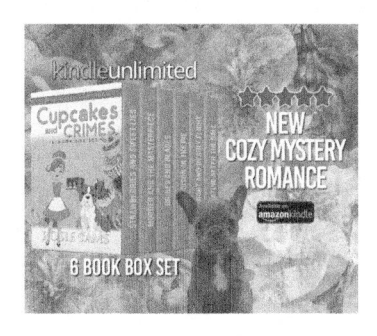

ALSO BY ROSIE SAMS & AGATHA PARKER

To be the first to find out when Rosie & Agatha release a new book and to hear about other sweet romance authors join the exclusive SweetBookHub readers club here.

∼

The Dog Detectives – The Beagle Mysteries

Sniffing out the Killer

On the Scent of Murder

Available FREE with KU
Or
Coming Soon

Bakers and Bulldogs Cozy Mystery Series:

Cupcakes and Crimes volume 1 - 6 Book Box Set

Books 1 to 6

**Cupcakes and Crimes volume 2 - 6 Book Box Set
Books 7 to 12**

Kidnapped at the Casino

Murder and the Magician

Wedding Dresses and Deadly Messes

Dying to Retire

The Stylist and the Deadly Cut

The Murder in the Motel

The Pushing in the Pond

If you enjoyed this book, Rosie and Agatha would appreciate it if you left a review on Amazon or Goodreads

Printed in Great Britain
by Amazon.co.uk, Ltd.,
Marston Gate.

Printed in Great Britain
by Amazon